I0571102

Sanjay's Essay

Sanjay's Essay

On What It's Like To Be Young Today

By Shyam Gohel

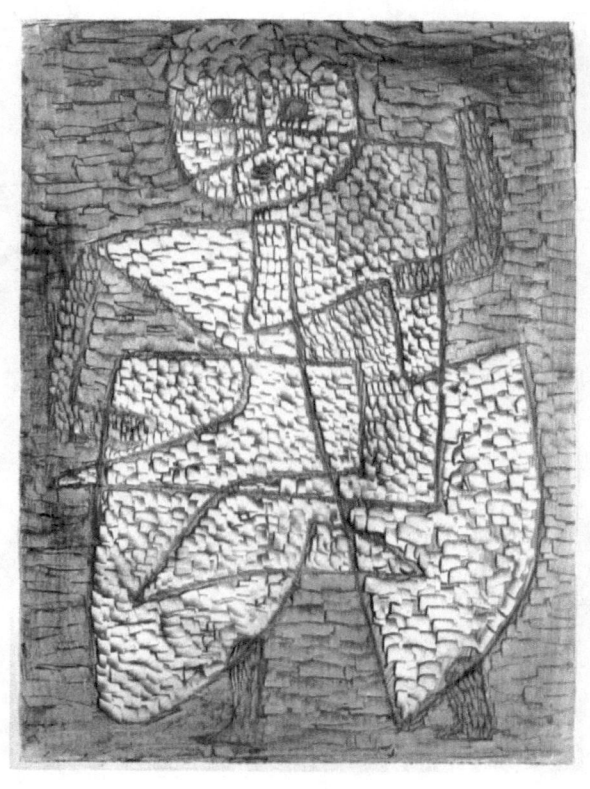

Copyright © 2025 Shyam Gohel

All rights reserved.

ISBN 979-8-9985022-8-6

Table of Contents

Introduction
by Shyam Gohel

1. Every once in a while, a young person is saying something, and you find yourself thinking alongside this young person as an equal.

Of course, this happens all the time with very young children. For example, three months ago a four-year-old child of a new friend of mine asked, "What is caffeine?"—and we were all struggling to answer this question, not only for the child but also for ourselves and each other. This is *not* what I'm speaking about.

What I am speaking of is a strange kind of connection a person my age makes with a much younger person at the level of thought, which changes the way the older person views their relationship. This is what happened to me at the age of forty-three, reading the following essay by sixteen-year-old Sanjay.

2. Since the pandemic, I have been giving private tuition lessons in the arts, in Morris County, New Jersey, in English literature and composition.*

---

* It hurts me to have been involved in the exchange of knowledge for money. Exchanging knowledge for money is a dishonest practice. But this is not the place for this discussion.

The object of the lessons is to promote critical thinking among young people before they reach their young adult years.

Critical thinking is a series of skills:

i.   Observing our patterns of thinking, speaking, and acting
     What do I believe?

ii. Questioning our beliefs
     Why do I believe what I believe?

iii. Evaluating our beliefs
     Am I right? Are my beliefs good for me and my relationships with others?

iv. Being open to what seem like strange and alien forms of beliefs
     Do I listen with care and understanding to all the implicit theories and social practices that come my way in the ordinary conversations and interactions of everyday life?

3. Sanjay was a student of mine.

It is easy for a teacher to *pose* questions to a student, either borrowing the style of his or her own teachers and mentors in life, or borrowing questions from his or her own life.

It is easy for a teacher to *answer* the questions of a student.

It is *not* easy for a teacher to stand by and watch a student start to think critically about a whole set of matters that do not come up every day anymore for the teacher, either because of older age, or because younger people are facing directly what only comes up indirectly for the teacher.

It's not easy, because the student is beginning to learn the great extent to which passion (emotional nature) and character (moral nature) play a role in our everyday education.

At this point, the teacher must let the student begin to learn in a much different, more substantive way—that is, through lived experience—and say, "You're ready to fly, Sanjay. Live well. All knowledge is in the heart. When the heart gets overheated, use the brain to cool down."

4. I wish for all of you to read Sanjay's essay. He wrote it as a long response to an open-ended assignment that had the prompt:

Remember the personal writing style of Pascal's *Pensées*, Descartes' *Meditations*, Rousseau's *Reveries*, or Plato's *Apologia*.

These authors were writing about their personal concerns and also the social issues of *their* time.

Write on any series of topics of your choice in your own style that are of *your* time.

Sanjay did not write this essay in a classroom indoors. We had gone for an outing on this day. Our scenery for the essay-assignment was the Great Swamp National Wildlife Refuge in nearby Basking Ridge.

5. A note on Sanjay's overall method.

I believe Sanjay had in mind Montaigne's "To the Reader" from *Essais*, which we had recently read together. Montaigne writes, "Therefore, Reader, I myself am the subject of my book." Sanjay also believed in the mystic procedure of reading the first sentence of everything—book, chapter, paragraph—to get a gist of what's going on in the entire work:* therefore, I'm sure he had in mind Montaigne's first sentences of Book 1, Chapter 1—"The most common way of softening the hearts of those we have offended once they have us at their mercy with vengeance at hand is to move them to commiseration and pity by our submissiveness. Yet flat contrary means, bravery and steadfastness and resolution, have sometimes served to produce the same effects"*—which is to say that Sanjay is writing a

---

* I myself observe the other mystic practice. I often read the last things first. First, I'll flip through the index, then the acknowledgments, endnotes, footnotes, then the epigraphs, and so on. (What we want to write about, in the beginning, doesn't turn out to be what we actually say at the end of the day.)

* As mentioned above, Sanjay, like many young people, looked to the first sentences of written pieces to quickly get an idea of

personal essay, a public confession, and an invitation card for further thought and thinking. Let me explain:

Sometimes when you begin to write, you already find yourself at a *deficit*.

Writing about oneself, especially—writing one's opinions, fragmentary as they often are—is to feel like one is already committing *an offense* against the true topics of the day, for example, political strife, war, environmental health, injustices in society, and troubles at home.

Sometimes *the way out of such deficit* is submissiveness.

But sometimes submissiveness looks a lot like *the courage to challenge our own thoughts and thinking*, i.e., to steady oneself before one begins a more important task— to first make a personal resolution—and then to struggle,

---

what the whole work is about. Therefore, he may also have had in mind Montaigne's first sentence of Book 2, Chapter 1: "Those who strive to account for a man's deeds are never more bewildered than when they try to knit them into one whole and to show them under one light, since they commonly contradict each other in so odd a fashion that it seems impossible that they should all come out of the same shop," or the first sentences of Book 3, Chapter 1: "No one is free from uttering stupidities. The harm lies in doing it meticulously. That [the meticulousness] does not apply to me. My trifles escape me with as little gravity as they deserve. Good luck to them for that. I would part with them at once, however low their price. I do not buy and sell them for more than they weigh. I speak to my writing-paper exactly as I do the first man I meet."

clash, dispute, argue, and, thereby, learn.

So Sanjay writes about himself.

He writes—in the great tradition of the Essay—about what he does not know about himself.

He depends on us to become as vulnerable as he is on his writing-paper.

This is my belief.

6. The title of this book, the chapter headings, and chapter breaks are mine. Sanjay did not label or mark anything.

Unless otherwise noted, all the footnotes are mine.*

---

* *An appeal to the reader.* Give Sanjay a while to warm up. He gets more settled as he goes on, and he spells out his thoughts more completely. (I also interrupt the flow of his thought less as he goes on.) While writing the essay, Sanjay twice asked me if we could get up and walk for a while around the Refuge to have a change of scenery: once after writing Chapter 7, then again after writing Chapter 8. The reader will notice a slight change of tone at these places.

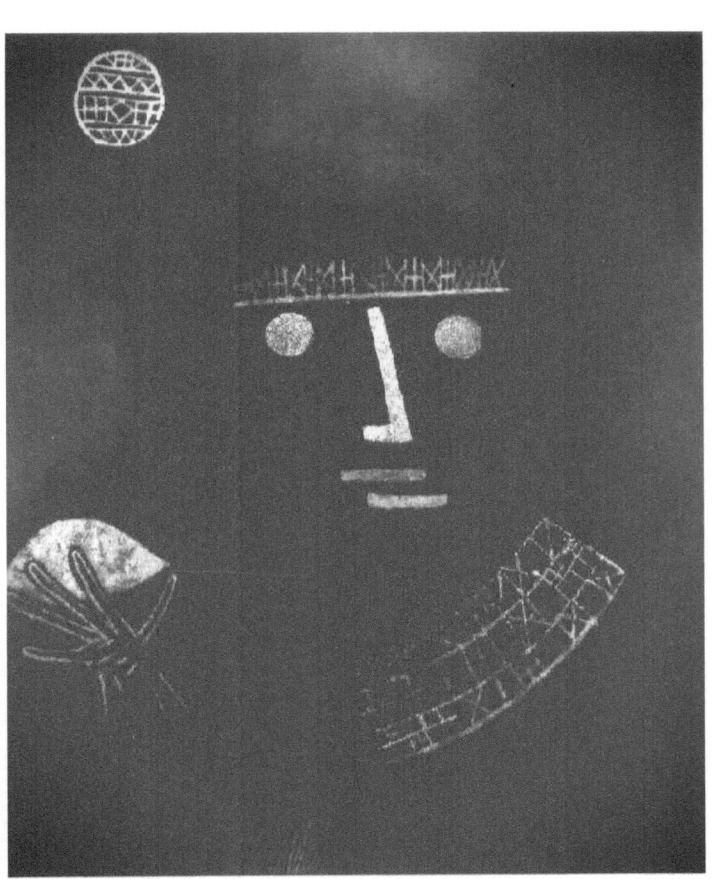

The Essay

I shall introduce myself, dear readers.

My name is Sanjay, which means "hero," "someone totally victorious," "warrior."

It is a totally outrageous name, isn't it?

What if you met someone whose name was Hero, Total Victory, or Warrior?

But such are the names of my old country.

I cannot help it.

I almost wish I am able to give it up someday.

But perhaps names are just words devoid of their natural meaning, and are sort of like titles or appointments or nominations.

Perhaps I can't wait to meet this Hero, Victorious, Warrior (that I am).

Perhaps I am afraid to meet this person (that I am).

Perhaps I am afraid I won't be able to recognize this future person as me anymore.

Such is fate, I suppose: you can run but you can't hide.

Today, July 7, 2025, I am all right.

I'm hoping it's the same with all of you, dear readers.

Gender

I am to say my pronouns at this time.

And I am perfectly willing to do so as a political statement or as evidence of allyship with the trans, genderqueer, gender non-conforming communities.

He/him/his.

But as a matter of inner expression, I do not feel he/him/his.

I feel that their announcements say absolutely nothing about me or my gender feelings.

I come to he/him/his as a matter of process of elimination.

Since I have no right to use she/her/hers or they/them/theirs—as appealing as these sound to me*— I am left with what I am left with.

The sounds of she/her or they/them are much prettier to my ear.

---

* It's *appealing* because solidarity is more active than allyship.

I like the sounds of "sh," "er," "ey," "em," don't you?

But I have no right.

I do not have the right to stand as—imitate—another, who I am not; I have only the right to stand "with" and "alongside."

I do not have a strong connection with my own gender.

I find it—not maleness but gender itself—oppressive.

I suppose that is the point?

Being misgendered—not once or twice, not even once or twice a day, but *all the time, for all time*—is oppressive.

Is it not that gender itself is oppressive?

Is "she" or "they" not a way to signify that a person is outside of the gender-oppression game?*

---

* I can see Sanjay's idea here in the following two ways, both of which result in the same scenario: **(1)** Taking a wide historical lens, to be *queer* has been thought to be unidentifiable *within/inside* the gender game (*queer* is odd, strange, i.e., abnormal, away from the normal, separated or departed from the norm); so queerness stood *outside the limits of* conventional gender; thereby, queerness *defined the limits* of traditional gender identification; therefore the norms *need to exclude* queerness; therefore norms *need* queerness; *but nowadays,* queer people do not want to play this role anymore in service of the norms; to be queer is nowadays to break the norms *from the outside,* where queerness has been happily banished. How does a person break the norms from the outside? By contending

Is it not a shorthand to say: "I am not who you say I

---

with this unidentifiable *power* that is within every person: this unidentifiable *power of life, desire, need* that we all struggle with; by embracing the fact that there is something inside us— call it soul or divinity, call it *Die Verneinung des Willens* (Schopenhauer), call it *Bejahung* (Nietzschean affirmation, "the joyous affirmation of the play of the world and of the innocence of becoming, the affirmation of a world of signs without fault, without truth, and without origin which is offered to an active interpretation"), call it *Todestrieb* (Freud)—that resists all stillness, convention, and self-agreement. The notion of queerness is that since "definitions belong to the definers, not the defined" (Toni Morrison, *Beloved*), queerness will not define itself, *or it will define itself as undefined* and undefinable, unidentifiable; and, thereby, *norms can no longer define themselves by prohibiting* something that cannot be defined. Norms break from the outside. Q.E.D. **(2)** Or, to take a strategy closer to modern times—say, since the publication of *Gender Trouble* by Judith Butler—to identify as gender queer is to introduce *within* gender norms a new type of category that the old way of thinking cannot handle (i.e., classify) or simply dislikes—dislikes because queerness is changing the "rules" and boundaries *by playing* by the rules, by introducing within the category of gender an element that *belongs to* and *yet negates* the set of perceived norms. In any case, Sanjay does not believe that queerness wants to be another category like its fellow categories male and female: that is a fantasy of the old ways, as if queerness were identified by relation to the old ways. Queerness wants to be its own thing; it prefers *not to participate* in the old ways. In a way that echoes many other questions of our day, queerness has always been and has always existed quite richly, with its own understandings of joy, friendship, and flourishing (*eudaimonia*)—and all it's asking for nowadays is not to be killed or harmed in body and mind for being and existing.

am"?

Are not "she" and "they" ways to say "I," "me," "mine," and "keep your hands off me"?*

I'll put all my cards on the table.

I may not be the best person to comment on this issue.

I have no concept or feeling of myself, let alone a gendered one.

I do not know how I feel, look, or act.

I do not feel like my body.

I am not talking about anatomy; I am talking about the living body, the weight, the shapes (curves, lengths), the texture, the plumpness, the toughness.

I feel like my body says nothing about me.

Not even my eyes.

Not even my hands.

Not even the sounds of my voice.

My body says nothing at all.

---

* Sanjay will come back to this idea when he talks about romance and the body at the end of this essay. I believe that he is speaking politically here. It becomes more complicated, as he'll say later, when someone loves you and accepts you and puts her hands on you without trying to change or control you.

My body, I feel, takes away from whatever I am trying to be?

My body is like a fact.

I am a question.

I am a searcher.

I am an arrow spinning around the entire world.

I am Jupiter, Saturn, Uranus, and Neptune: *pure*

atmosphere, a whole mood, a gas giant, something between liquid and a collection of ice rocks; I am pressure, temperature, a giant storm larger than all of the Earth.

If I could take off my body, I would try. (Someone who has an appointment with total victory always gives it a try.)

I have heard that pure fun, play, and joy are when you lose yourself and lose track of time.

Like, when you're listening to music, walking with a friend, taking a walk with your dog (my dog's name is Nyla, which, funny enough, also means "winner"), daydreaming, imagining, thinking, remembering, or, perhaps, praying.

All good things, it seems to me, make the feeling of my body less heavy on me.

It's not *a* good feeling.

It's a feeling *of what is* good.

You know what I mean?

The feeling itself is a goodness, like a kindness, like a forgetting, like *being there* without the feeling of being anywhere.*

---

* *"Lose yourself and lose track of time"* and *"my body less heavy on me"*: Sanjay is here quoting from memory a book we read together that said that sleep is not rest. Real rest, the book said,

I am not speaking about causing harm to the body.

I am speaking about feeling at odds with myself.

I am speaking about things I am not sure of.

If you don't know what you're unsure of about yourself, just wait.

A bully will come and touch that nerve.

Bullying

A real bully—a bully who's really good at bullying— preys on the thing about yourself you're not sure of.

A bully reminds you that you are not even free to think about yourself the way you want to think about yourself.

---

is finding a good posture for yourself, breathing good, feeling that you are neither the body nor the mind (body, breath, and mind are three names for the same thing, the book said), and losing all sense of this small, small world you've created for yourself (i.e., worrying all the time, being pushed around and pulled into things) by thinking of the infinite, like the infinite sky, or the infinite ocean, e.g., while in meditation. This book said that each of us *is the ocean*. We are not waves that rise and fall as *part* of the ocean (like we hear on *The Good Place* or *The White Lotus*); each of us is the *whole, entire* ocean. (These are paradoxes of the infinite, which Sanjay enjoyed. It's like when Juliet says, "I wish but for the thing I have. My bounty is as boundless as the sea, my love as deep. The more I give to thee, the more I have, for both are infinite.")

You are in the hands of others.

Others can lay their hands on you.

How do you want these hands to be laid upon you?

A bully wants submission.

A bully wants you to be free only in submission to your fate (of being at the mercy of the bully).

In a certain way, the bully is right.

That's why being bullied is so confusing.

At some level, when you're being bullied, you think to yourself: "I deserve this." It's a very sad, very *tragic* thought, I'm sorry to say.

"I deserve *this*." What is the "this"? What do I, who am being bullied, deserve?

I'll come back to this question. But it* is similar to the young feeling (the idea inside me) that "I am not who you say I am."

"I am not what you say I am."

Every young person rebels this way: "I am not what

---

* "It" refers to the *structure* of how "I deserve this" is absolutely wrong but gets at something right, in the same way that the *structure* of "I am not who you say I am" is absolutely right but also gets something very wrong about the extent to which we are able to determine ourselves.

you say I am," and she's right.

But also, every young person feels: "I do not feel like me if *you* don't see all the conflict I feel."*

A loved one is someone who sees the struggles in me.

A bully sees the same, and presses on that tender feeling in me in order to cause pain.

It takes a lot to remind myself that a bully causes pain.

There's nothing noble about that.

A bully believes in the pervasiveness, the inescapability, the fatefulness, the commonness of pain.

I really am no match for my bullies.

They are much bigger and more powerful than me in body and tactics.

But I do not go down without a fight.

That's the best I can do, dear readers.

When I have no option but to fight and take a fall, I take that option, dear readers.

Some people tell me that making fun of a bully is no way to fight back. (It's unethical, they say.)

---

* The inner conflict is the grounds for rebellion, e.g., "I am not rebelling against *what* I'm rebelling against. I am rebelling against *you*, i.e., your power over me."

Some people tell me that I better be good and fair in a fight, lest I suffer the same fate as the bully, who believes in pain.

I don't know about all that.

I *do* know that comedy and humor—making fun— work miracles sometimes.

Somehow they take away from the bully the thing that the bully wants most.

Comedy touches that same sore spot we have about ourselves but without that punishing kind of pain.

Comedy says that things don't have to be the way they are.

By self-inflicted or self-targeted comedy or humor,* I say, "I know I'm not perfect. I wasn't trying to be perfect. I am trying to make myself good. You (the bully) are not perfect, either. Make yourself good, my friend (i.e., my enemy, my bully, my hated object, full of pain)."

By comedy or humor, I say, "None of this is real. You're after something in me that doesn't exist. You're literally bullying me for no reason."

Of course, a bully is not to be reasoned with.

That doesn't work.

---

* Self-deprecating humor.

You can talk to a bully but not talk a bully out of the bullying, after a certain point, in any case; and that point happens pretty fast, if you ask me.

A bully makes you feel like nothing will ever change.

A bully makes you feel like you'll never really be able to heal the things for which you're being picked on.

A bully makes you feel like you don't deserve to be who you are at the moment.

A bully makes you feel like you're not allowed to be *at all*.

I'm sorry to say this, but, at a certain point, there's no running away from a bully.

You'll have to confront your fears.

You'll have to do something, by yourself. (Friends can help. Of course, friends will help. Friendship is the opposite of pain.)

You'll have to be more courageous than you really are.

You'll have to let this idea of yourself go: that you are weak, that you can't do anything, that you can't accomplish anything, that you have no right to say anything, that you have no right to speak out, to fight back, to be someone, to be free.

I may not be the best person to comment on this issue.

People get bullied for their looks (attractiveness), size, weight, intelligence, wealth, abilities (social, athletic, and so on), color, body smell, family type, gender type, preferences in love and sexuality.

I don't believe any of these things are who we are.

I don't know how to say it.

A bully wants me to feel like I could wither up and die, because the bully is taking away from me something that shouldn't be taken away from me.

A bully wants to leave a wound on me that will not heal.

I don't believe there is anything like that, really.

As much as there are many things I cannot change about myself—*and* as much as there are many things that I won't change about myself just because someone says so (I'll do it if *I* want to)—most of those things are not worth keeping safe from harm in the first place, I feel.

That's just me.

I don't know how to say it, dear readers.

I don't want to say, "Don't let a bully hurt you," because I know how much it hurts.

But I am saying something like it.

What do you do about a bully?

How do you solve for bullying?

Perhaps, be less afraid.

Don't believe the bully.

Don't believe in that kind of pain: the kind of pain that just gets passed on from one person to another, because pain must hit a target, and that target happens to be you.

Let me stop talking about the bully, because the bully's

type of pain—which tries to convince you that you'll always be a victim—is hard to deal with *but not impossible.*

The bully preys upon our insecurities.

The bullying loses its particular sting when you know that you'll always have the power to heal yourself: don't give up on yourself.

Push back.

I want to talk about a different type of pain of being young.

There are some words and ideas that older people think we don't know about.

But we know about them.

We see them in people we know, people in our family.

We see them in ourselves, sometimes, perhaps: words and ideas like *depression* and *grief.*

Depression and Grief

Those're of a different type of pain.

That type of pain is about something that is lost.

Something that is gone, like an energy that has become

wasted away.

Depression is like heartbreak, grief is like heartache.

They both are feelings.

Depression feels like God has abandoned you.

Grief feels like God keeps reaching out to you to take away the things you love.

Both are feelings.

Depression is like your heart is out of joint.

Grief is like your heart doesn't know what it's for anymore.

Or depression is like your heart is a memory: something you used to have as the person you used to be.

And grief is like your heart is a memory: something you have and you don't know what to do with anymore without the persons and things with whom you used to spend time.

Depression and grief are not just any feelings. These are feelings that say, "We have no time counting down on the clock. We could stay here forever. You'd be a fool to try and change."*

---

* *"We have no time . . ."* is the feeling of depression and grief talking to the person who's hurting.

I think I have the right to talk about depression and grief, because I either know them myself, or I've seen them on my friends, or I see them virtually everywhere in so many people.

These feelings are different from all other ones because there's something about a loss of life, a loss of the feeling of life.

There's a loss of the sense of life.

There's a loss of the feeling of aliveness.

It's like you're in a relationship with a loss(-feeling).

Other feelings are like you're in a relationship with other people (or society at large) or with the work you're working on.

Depression and grief are like how you feel about your feelings.

It's like a disappointment in your feelings.

Feelings bring energy one way or another.

But with depression and grief, you're disappointed with all the energy of your feelings.

It's like you despise energy.

It's like all energy is too much energy ... for what? Just for it all to be depleted or taken away?

Why shall I go on living?

Why shall I go on living the same way I've been going on living?

Would I be able to, even if I wanted to?

Depression and grief take away from you the desire to have feelings at all.

They become whole moods and personalities, if you're not careful.

If you don't remember that they are, after all, feelings themselves, too.

I may not be the best person to comment on this issue.

There really is no *solution* solution.

Not everything has a solution.

I wouldn't even say that there's a remedy or resolution to depression and grief.

One thing* I know is that: things—including feelings, including people—don't always want to be looked at closely.

Sometimes you look at a thing, and it falls apart.

We don't like to look because it's scary.

---

* One possible remedy.

It's scary, because, sometimes, that thing is—most things are—terrifying.

It's terrifying, because you feel it has this power over you.

And you'd be right.

Things have a power over you when you feel like they're looking back at you—like you're in a relationship or something.*

It's like you're being caught in the eyes of this thing.

When grief has her eyes on you, it's a very alone feeling.

When depression has her eyes on you, it's like you're not there.

I don't know, but I imagine that when there's no solution to a feeling, there may be more than one way out.

Of course, one way to live with grief is to live with it.

This person is gone.

This friend is gone.

This companion is gone from life.

This time in my life is ended in my life.

I have gained, and I have lost.

It was a form of mercy or grace that I should have gained such a person, friend, companion, or time in my life in the first place: *why is it not a form of mercy or grace that I should have lost . . . ?***

---

* Think of when you were Sanjay's age and your love (or crush) feels your eyes on her: *it's literally a terrifying moment for the both of you!*

** The mercy or grace is that to have lost . . . is to have had . . .

How do mercies become despair?

Is there a rule that everything ends in despair?

I don't think so.

I know it feels that way.

But there's no rule about it.

It may take longer than you thought.

But a time may come.

A time may come when you feel like you've learned as much as you can from depression and grief: *a whole lot of nothing.*

There are times of suffering, and there are feelings of suffering: *I'm not so sure how wise suffering is.**

I'm not so sure how much suffering can teach.

(The opposite of suffering is not happiness: it's the feeling of life.)**

Some people say that suffering is "the great teacher."

What could we possibly learn from suffering?

That we expect too much?

---

* Sanjay is saying that suffering doesn't produce knowledge—neither practical knowledge nor ethical knowledge.
** Sanjay will talk about happiness later.

That the world doesn't owe us anything?

That not everything about us has to be successful?

Maybe, who knows.

I don't buy it.

In any case, there's no reason to have a love of suffering, as if it were a great teacher.*

I have no easy answer here.

Maybe there's something in being a little foolish about things.

If depression and grief say, "You'd be a fool to try and live again"—this may be the only way out: *take a risk, be a little less wise, be a tad reckless, and don't be unwilling to lose again at the end of it all.*

There are things worth living for.

There's someone just like you out there.

Someone who's hurting just like you.

Someone who's made it out.

I'm not asking for anything impossible.

---

* *Note by Sanjay:* I know a good teacher when I see one. A good teacher laughs. A good teacher cares. A good teacher asks you how you are. A good teacher has time for you. I can't make a whole list here. A good teacher does not ask you to suffer.

Carry your hurt with you, why not.

Life has this thing about it: *if it goes on for a while, it makes more of it.*

Without crushing anything down, there will be more of what it is.

It does it without trying.

I don't find the feeling of life to be a hot, explosive power.

Life is a kind of power that has no power over anything else (certainly not death, certainly not loss of life).

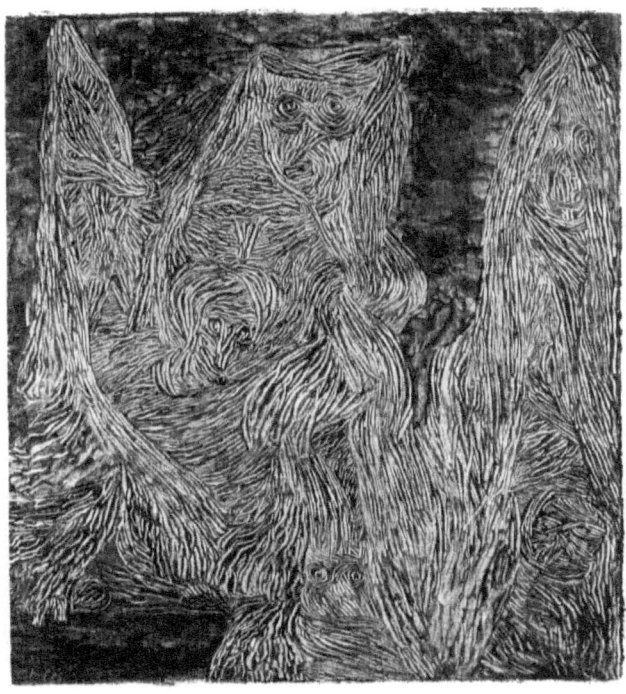

I have heard Shyam recite a poem many, many times:

"You may be weaker than the whole world,

but you are always stronger than yourself."

"You may be less powerful than the whole world,

but you are always more powerful than yourself."

I don't know what it means, exactly.

But I have a clue about it.

I can tell you what it's *not*.

Health, Wellness, Happiness

It's not this "need to be happy" attitude that people like to talk to me about.

It's not about the kind of "health and wellness" that everyone likes to talk about, as if happiness could be measured and studied in a lab, as if there could be a science of happiness, like the science of baking a cake or dissecting the heart of a frog.

I have to be careful here, because I can get hot about this.

I don't think the goal of life is to be happy.

I don't think we ought to be as concerned with wellness and everyday mental health as we're being sold today.

The very idea that people make money off selling happiness and health is suspicious to me.

Nothing is simpler than to know that happiness comes from doing the right thing.

That's it.

It's as simple as that.

Sometimes the *doing* of the right thing is difficult.

It takes courage and honesty.

Sometimes *knowing* the right thing is difficult.

That's the work.

None of this has to do with happiness.

None of this has to do with being true to yourself.

There is no happiness stored away inside yourself from your early years of innocence.*

The innocence of children (younger than me) is that they do not hesitate to act.

Children take action. They go after their desires. They

---

* Sanjay is saying that happiness is not your authentic self. There is no authentic self. Every teenager knows this. Don't think teenagers don't know anything.

play. They test. They learn consequences. They figure out what is good for the body, what hurts, what is what (knowledge), what they want, and what makes them feel good.

Happiness is the outcome of action.

That's it.

It's as simple as that.

Happiness is the outgrowth of action, like something you didn't know would feel so good if you did the right thing.

Happiness is the real thing—don't get me wrong.

It's just not everything it's made out to be.

It's not everything you want it to be.

Happiness is something that comes back to you after you've done something.

I could tell you ten different things that are more worth your time than striving after happiness.

(1) Goodness is more important than happiness. Doing good is not always smooth. I can be good only by doing you good. There is just no other way to do it. And so, there is some feeling of humility in doing the right thing: I can sometimes put your needs and your wants above mine. That's just how happiness works sometimes. You

give up your happiness to do the right thing. You postpone your happiness for the sake of something better than your happiness. What is good for you may not be good for everyone. What is good for her may not be good for someone else. (2) There is good stuff in being torn up about all this. This is how we are in the world. There is no Good for everyone. There is not even a good that is clear for myself: sometimes being a good brother means being a not-so-good son; sometimes being a good friend

means being a not-so-good brother. A person is many things all at the same time. Sometimes we get at odds with ourselves. We get torn up and divided against ourselves. Things get ambiguous. You don't know what to do. You have to act: should I protect my friend by lying to my teacher? Sometimes yes, sometimes no. You have to come to some decision you might regret: should I lose a friend and stick to the truth? Sometimes yes, sometimes no. It's all ambiguous. This difficult type of decision-making is more worthwhile than happiness, for sure; trust me. (3) Sometimes regret and grief and loss are better than happiness. They mean you cared. (4) Truth is a hundred percent better than happiness. I've heard that we all have some core values that we believe in, and that sticking it out and living truly to these core values save us from a lot of inner conflict. I completely believe this. But sticking it out sometimes involves a lot of pain. It involves real belief. It involves something like real faith. (5) Faith is better than happiness; and faith is never easy. Faith is always tested. Being tested is better than being happy. Being tested means that you have to choose your core values every single time. That is not easy. Being free is not easy. Having faith is not easy. It's almost not even a free feeling. It feels like you *have to* do it, if you are to recognize yourself, live with yourself, feel good about yourself, as if you were trying to do the right thing out of a deep love for something other than yourself. (6) Isn't thinking about things other than yourself—and your happiness—better than happiness? (7) Love is better than happiness. Unselfishness is better than happiness. Not neglecting other people is better than happiness. Doesn't all this sound very difficult? Doesn't all this sound too messy for a happiness lab or happiness science? Love is about something that you cannot prove even exists! Think about it. What is it about this thing or this person that makes you love her? What is that special something? If you can tell me all about it, I wouldn't believe you.

Love is when you believe in this thing even when the whole world says otherwise. Love is when you can't convince anyone else about what you see and how you see it. Love is when love gets to work. Love is when you can't quite get a grip on it. Love is when you're afraid to even reach out and touch it—you don't want to harm it or change it (for the worse) with your touch. Love is real

when you feel it increasing at almost every moment. Love is only known by feeling. Love can never be caught in your thoughts or imaginations. Love is when you know that you have to stop talking about love, because the words do not do—the words do not do justice to love. You will have to stop fighting for your love in words at some point, and be quiet and get to work.

(8) Friendship is another thing that is better than

happiness. I really don't hear much about friendship at all. I hear a lot about making connections and opening up and getting vulnerable, as if it were an easy thing. It is not easy at all. Anyone in a friendship knows how much pain and strife there is in there. The sharing of pain and strife almost *is what friendship is.* You go through all the emotions in a friendship. I don't think happiness has anything to do with friendship. A good friend lets you have all the feelings. This is not as gentle as it seems. A good friend sometimes corrects or cancels your feelings. A good friend judges your feelings. A good friend tells you the truth, plain and simple. If a friend keeps you happy, get suspicious, because a good friend should want what is *good* for you. I really believe that this "happiness culture" of "health" and "wellness" I hear about so much is afraid of having feelings. What I'm saying may sound like the opposite of what they're saying. They will tell you that happiness is all about having healthy feelings, like gratitude, kindness, curiosity (interest, motivation), embrace the small moments, accept yourself, be good to yourself. I am not talking about these feelings. They don't sound like happiness to me. I'm not against happiness—don't get me wrong. I'm saying that happiness is not a product you can get by making a few adjustments here and there. Happiness is what happens after you live the entirety of your full emotional life. (You can't aim directly for happiness.) You can't talk yourself into having feelings.

You can't talk yourself out of unhappy feelings. You can't analyze a feeling and let it fall to bits at your feet by inspecting it to death. You have to go through it. Feelings want to be felt. If they're not felt, they'll clot. (9) Feeling your feelings is something better than happiness. And, if I may say, there's a lot to feel about that is unhappy. Sometimes an outburst of emotion—like, anger at the fact that school shootings are a normal part of life (the fact that I have to go through metal detectors to get to school), anger at the fact that our politics is as uncivilized at it was 250 years ago, anger at having to save up money to go to the doctor or a hospital, and the sadness, fear, anxiety, and grief that follow or produce these angers—has an emotional effect that is healthier than happiness. I just get afraid that *happiness* as it's being sold to us is a version of "enjoy the little that you have in your life." As if it were: "avoid suffering." As if the goal of life were "be satisfied with your lot." As if our fate were not always being reversed. As if life itself were not a struggle to become free. Free from what? From this trap of personal happiness, personal health, and personal wellbeing. There are so many of us—*us*—who suffer undeserved misfortune. We fall into terrible adversity. Let the person who is happy give up her happiness and dive into this adversity. (10) Such adversity is better than happiness. We feel this adversity because we are human. We are not humans to be studied in a happiness lab. We are humans with terrible, tragic faults, fallibilities and vulnerabilities.

Suffering an undeserved fate is almost what it means to be human. I see this everywhere in our movies and TV shows. I don't think that the people who talk about "happiness" know what strange creatures we are. We are full of divine (generous) and human (beholden) characteristics: therefore, we are some kind of monster of

the divine and human. We sometimes act with a godlike nature (and the gods never experience happiness, because they are not obligated to enjoy, they are not obligated to act—they perform miracles); and we sometimes are terribly separated from our higher nature; we act as if the fact of school shootings and political control over the nature and function of our bodies should not disturb our happiness. Most of all, the happiness industry wants to avoid feelings of guilt and shame and the endless back-and-forth of making decisions for (the good of) each other.

What if happiness were off the table?

What would we do then?

How would we act?

What if the management of pleasure and pain weren't a thing?

What if, while we lived, we lived to do something good for someone else, even at the cost of the routines that protect our happiness?

Happiness comes from the feeling of having lived a meaningful life, doesn't it?

It is *personal* insofar as no one else can act or make decisions for you.

What will you do in life? Only you can decide.

Sometimes you have to make an impossible choice.

There are many impossible choices you'll have to make.

I think most people will agree that it is better to suffer than do the wrong thing.

Sometimes—not often but sometimes—that's the only choice you have.

I may not be the best person to comment on all this.

I get too worked up.

I apologize for that.

A writer should never write angry.

It just doesn't sound good.

It's off-putting.

A rant is nice to hear when it's done by a comedian.

A comedian puts distance between herself and the issue at hand.

Laughter—and the pleasures of laughter—is the goal of the comic.

She challenges all these things about everyday life that we just accept as they are and always will be.

She talks about life.

She talks about suffering and the absurdities of it all in

the context of life and the fullness of life.

Laughter is a sign of affection, after all.

Social Media

I can now make a series of confessions.

I know what it's like to be young today, but there's a lot I do not know about what it means to be young today.

I'm not on social media.

I tried, but I found that I wasn't posting anything. I wasn't sharing anything.

I was lurking.

I was around.

I was watching what others do, and how they presented themselves.

I couldn't tell if a person's social media image was her true self or virtual self.

In any case, I found that I was mostly in the habit of stalking my friends, people I knew and saw every day—for sure once a week—on Snap or IG.

I didn't like that feeling.

I was obsessing over what Kayla was doing, and who

she interacted with.

We were good friends—more than friends—for a long time, and I messed it up.

We never got to talk about it.

Overnight, we stopped talking.

It was a misunderstanding.

This was maybe less than two months ago.

Knowing what I know now, I'm sure that it was always going to end this way.

There's no other way for it to have ended, given who I was, how clueless I was, how much I do not know about how to be more than friends with someone like Kayla, and given who she was, how shy she was, or used to be.

I'm sure she's the same person.

It's only been two months.

But things change, or seem to change, overnight sometimes.

I mostly use my phone for YouTube and WhatsApp, mostly for music and shorts and talking with some of my family—one aunt and one cousin—back in India. But I don't use these apps like social media.

I use them like a radio or messages.

I'm embarrassed.

I know.

I confess.

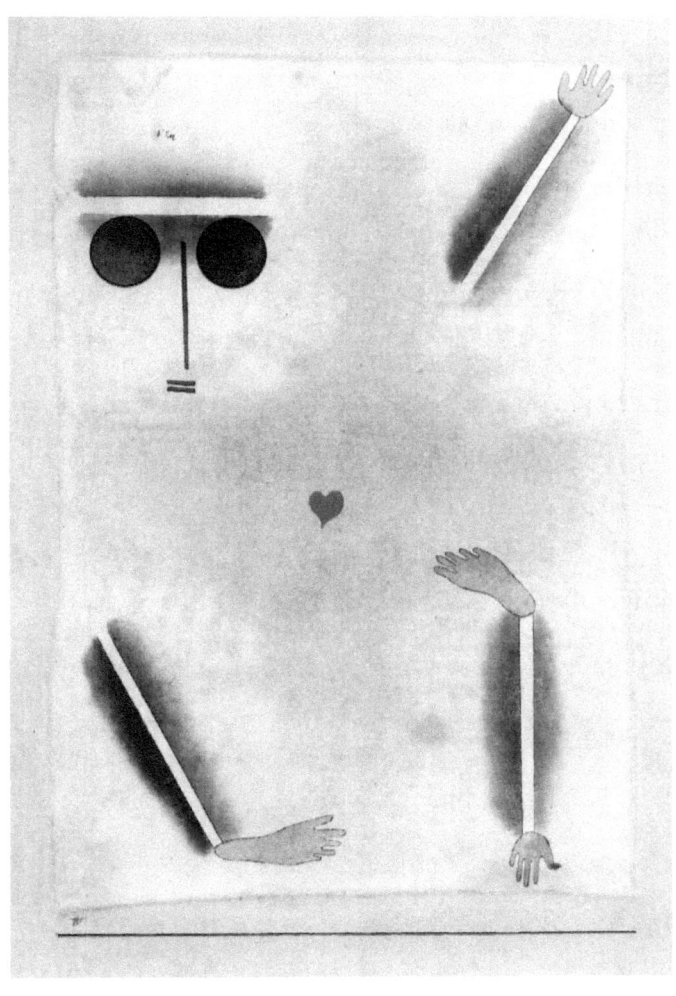

I use the notes app on my phone, photos rarely, and a browser. That's it, really.

I know this is not typical for someone my age.

I suppose I miss out on a lot of things.

I'm not sure what they are.

I'm scared of making a wrong move on my phone, if I get connected to people.

I'm scared, perhaps, of showing too much of myself, or, really, in reality, too much of someone that I am not.

I don't know why, but I feel myself more honest, or less dishonest, with pen and paper or typing on the tablet.

If I'm writing an essay, I'll turn off autocomplete, so I really have a blank page, and no one but myself to fill it in.

It's one reason I liked the Montaigne essays, even though I understood none of them.

Montaigne wrote freely.

There was no formula.

He wrote about himself.

He wrote parts of himself.

He attempted to write parts of himself.

He didn't always get it right, either.

He was having a conversation with himself.

He was thinking out loud without worrying if he was getting himself right or not.

He said he was making paintings of himself in his essays.

I like that idea.

He painted thoughts.

But he didn't write a diary.

I imagine that social media is a kind of diary.

But social media is a strange kind of diary that has the same formula for all of us.

I suppose I won't have a diary for myself.

I do regret that I won't have many photos of myself.

Sometimes I look good and wish I had kept some evidence of that.

But I am not sure something like that would bring Kayla back.

Perhaps saying something to her would be a start—not to get her back, but to show her that I have no hard feelings about the misunderstanding, *and that it was a misunderstanding, not an injury or betrayal of mine upon her!*

Now that I think of it, I could say, next time I see her, "I'm sorry I haven't been talking to you. I've been scared to talk to you."

But I probably won't.

I don't know what to tell you.

It's as if there's been this tragic ending to our relationship, and at the same time the worst part about it is that I'm still playing a role in it (the tragedy) by not saying anything.

It's like it was fated to happen—given me and given her—and yet I did it with my own hands.

I played my part in it as if I had no control over it.

I let the ending happen to me.

I let it happen, I suppose.

That's the worst kind of ending.

In any case, I cannot say much about social media.

I ended up telling you about Kayla.

Please don't show these words to her.*

---

* Sanjay and Kayla have given their permission to publish this essay as it was written.

Money

The next confession I have to make is that I don't know how money works.

It seems you need money for everything.

You can't eat, sleep somewhere, or get a Band-Aid without money.

You need money to survive.

It's more valuable than survival itself. I don't get that. People can't survive without any money.

Whatever I want or need, first I need money.

I don't know how money can be so powerful that it defines (limits) what I can want and what I can afford to need.

Art is expensive.

Sport is expensive.

Music is expensive.

I have time and energy, but first I need to make money with them; then I can have all the art, sport, and music I can pay for.

What about love?

How much does that cost?

I don't know.

An arm and a leg?

No, seriously, I may not be the best person to comment on this issue.

Even if I have feelings for someone, money is part of the relationship.

I not only need money; I'm ashamed to say that money probably shapes whom I find desirable and attractive and worthy of my love.

It's like I can't even have my own feelings and experiences without its influence on me.

I would like to think that I have basic human needs that are fulfilled by people and their traditions* that keep me alive and healthy and more: they teach me about work, artistry in our works, dignity, friendship, spending time together, having fun, making art, creative expressions of all kinds, caring for each other, caring for people who need caring of different kinds.

Over and above some of these basic needs, I have my own *wants*.

---

* Our institutions, e.g., schools, libraries, community centers, parks, and public transportation.

Maybe I want to stand out.

Maybe I want to push the limits of what a human body can do, or want to decorate the human body in various beautiful ways.

Maybe I want to read more, be alone, think, and talk more about what I'm thinking.

Maybe I want to travel and explore.

These are all desires I have: when my wants are over and above my needs, then I have desires.

All this is emotional work as it is.

These are all educations in feelings and relationships.

But the money aspect of it all makes it all seem dull and

boring, kind of blasé.*

It's like we're already born terribly indebted and in need.

We are not born free, I'm sorry.

I have never felt free like that.

I do the best I can, given what I know, and all this schooling I get I get because it'll get me out of the debt I owe to my mother for all the love and care she's given me from the start—or my parents or guardians, whatever form of family we get when we're terribly young.

It's something I cannot repay of course.

It used to be that we didn't think of it as payment or repayment but debt.

In the very old days—correct me if I'm wrong—this was the idea of (original) sin, of moral debt, or mortal debt, the condition of being weak and dependent and demanding that one's existence be accompanied by pleasure of some kind or other.

Sin is like this guilt-like feeling we all have just for existing sometimes.

It's like we're always being reminded that we're not as perfect as we've been meant to be in the image of God.

---

* Unimpressive beyond its monetary (market) value.

We're not as forgiving (as God). We cannot relieve each other of our dependence on each other—only God can do that.

I don't want to talk about sin, though. People have funny ideas about it. I don't believe in sin, but I know the feeling of starting off with the feeling that I must be doing something wrong or something must be wrong with me. Why do I require so much more than what I need? Why do I have desire? Why do I desire? What do I desire? What do I want?

What do people want from me?

They mostly seem to want to educate me badly, i.e., correct me in all the ways they believe I'm flawed.

But I do not need that type of education.

I need the kind of education that makes me independent with regard to paying off my everyday debts every day, more or less, by accepting that you and I, and everyone else, are dependent on each other.

I need the kind of education that can't be bought with money.

I want human experiences in this world, the kind of experiences that touch my arm to your arm and my leg to yours.

What is the value of a human life?

Forget about how much money we have. Rather, what do we spend our money on?

What do we do with all our time and energy?

It may not be a bad thing that teenagers live in a utopian world.

At least teenagers have a sense of a world with other people with real arms and legs who are allowed to have wants above and beyond their basic needs.

We don't want to grow up to be isolated, with all our money to ourselves (—not until we grow older, I suppose. And what would have changed between now and old? Money takes over? It becomes the number one want and need, and tells us what to want and need in return?).

Teenagers are usually not imagining an ideal society that has no shot at being realized. We're not that stupid.*

We're also not usually imagining a future world of all pleasure, all fun and games, at the expense of basic human feelings, e.g., sharing what we can when we can with others at the expense of our pleasure.

We're utopian in the sense that we don't believe that

* "It's also the way in which imagination fosters *real* possibilities. If you can't imagine it, you can't have it." Toni Morrison, interview with Literary Arts, 1992.

this can just go on the way it's going now.

We're not going to be able to survive and live with ourselves if money decides who lives and breathes, eats and has shelter, learns and is able to grow with a sense of personal purpose and fulfilment.

We don't want to just imagine a utopia and have it built for us.

We want to build a space where there are no more excuses for why some (large) number of people cannot afford to live.

Money, right now, seems to tell us even who is a good person or a bad person.

I do not understand that at all.

Not at all.

You'll ask me, "What would you have us do?" because I'm young and want the world to be less punishing.

I suppose, I'll ask right back, "Do you know that you're already living in *someone else's* utopia? Art, music, sport, politics, morality are all valued by *money's* utopia. Maybe money itself—*its* utopia—would be better served if *it* had a notion of original sin, *its* indebtedness to us, to life, *its* mortal weakness, *its* transgressions against our human laws and arms and legs."

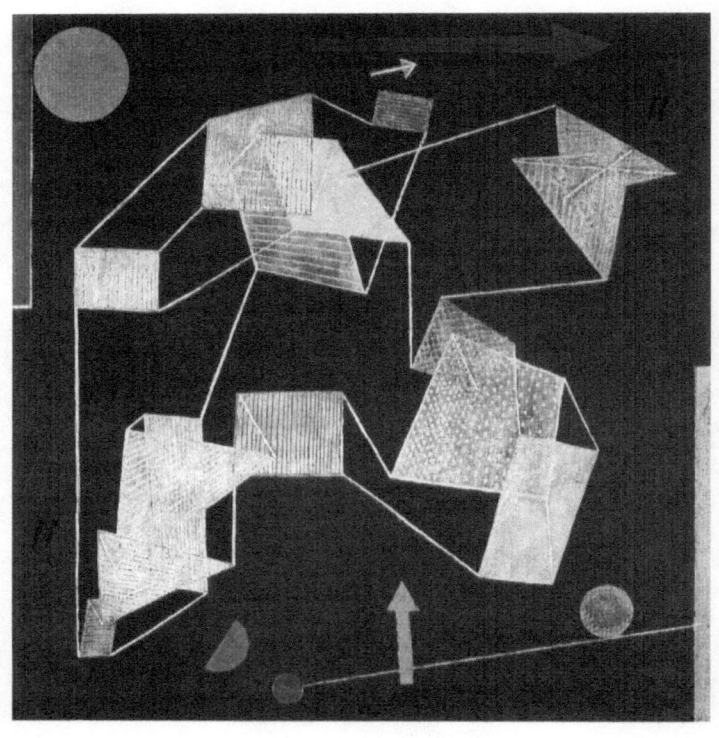

I don't like to write while I get worked up and upset or mad.

That never reads well.

But I feel like *freedom* is a word that I've been hearing a lot in the past few years. I don't think you can be free just by yourself. I admit that money is a way to freedom. Yes. Fine. Of course. You can use money everywhere to get anything. You can send money to people when you can't get to them. You can receive money and use it however you want. *But this freedom that money makes possible isn't the freedom by which we mean "freedom."* Let me ask another question: "What do we do with all this freedom we have (by money)?" People have *worked* for me to be this free. People who have come before me have *suffered without the freedom* I have now, and they went through great pains—physical pains, bodily aches and agony, and also heartache—simply trying to live their lives and move freely, speak freely, make money not through dishonest means, and they were forced, as it were, to think about how to get themselves free. No one wants to go through all that. People who work and suffer for our freedom do it out of necessity, in a way. They are forced to fight for their lives, not just figuratively and politically, but literally. (This is something of the feeling of guilt I was writing about earlier; it feels like a huge unpayable debt to have the freedom I have now. *It feels wrong to enjoy it: that's the feeling of original sin, that there's something wrong at the very beginning of my life*, that I have the things I have today because others have suffered for it.) I have seen videos where there are children my age and younger than me in this country on Edmund Pettus Bridge fighting not just for themselves but for the social conditions in this whole country to change.

I hear about money and happiness.

Can money bring happiness?

What about money and freedom?

I hear some people say that freedom means having no fear.

I hear some people say that freedom is having nothing left to lose.

I hear some people say that it's having friends and loved ones who care about you deeply.

Sometimes I hear that it's the freedom to change and create and create change.

It's true that I don't know how to reconstruct the whole world to be free of all the things that make life unfair and borderline intolerable.

I don't know why life is sometimes so beautiful for so many people, and at the same time so painful and hopeless for so many more people.

I don't plan on making sense of it all right now.

I also am not saying that we need to fulfil the hopes and dreams of anyone who came before us, or who will come after us, as a society—that doesn't seem like freedom, that feels like not taking responsibility for who we are today.

We don't have to judge ourselves according to anyone else, past or future.

I think we like talking about freedom, because there're no personal judgments about it.

I'm not any better or worse for it.

I'm just free.

That's all.

That's the good news, and the bad news.

Because freedom doesn't tell you what to do.*

All you end up with is having to deal with your life.

Your life stops at you.

And my life stops at me.

But freedom doesn't like to stay free.

I don't know how to say it.

Freedom wants to get entangled in things, wants to do something with itself**—partly for the reason that freedom is totally scary, partly for the reason that freedom wants to find pleasure, wants to find someone who is on the other side of you.

I'll get to the idea of "love" in a bit, because love and freedom go together. (Love is the opposite of money.)

But the first real feeling of freedom—and you have to agree that this is terrifying—is the freedom to find

---

* That's the bad news: freedom doesn't tell you what to do.
** "The function of freedom is to free someone else." Toni Morrison, Barnard College commencement speech, 1979.

pleasure with somebody.

There are no rules here.

No real rules of nature or of authorities of any kind.

Sex and Romance

I won't talk too much about sex, because I'm really not the right person to talk much about it.

I don't know enough about it.

And no one who's not my age wants to hear what someone my age has to say about it.

It gets borderline creepy if you're too interested in what goes on here, even if you did want to know what young people think about sex nowadays.

I can say safely that choosing who you want to have physical closeness with (romance, emotional attraction) is a freedom that contains a lot of other freedoms (of the body).

Sex is more or less about being desired.

I want to feel desired.

I want someone to want me and not need me.

I want someone to not get anything out of me other

than me.

That's what makes it intimate (and scary).

There's very little there.

There are only bodies.

What is made is made by bodies.

The body has a power of its own.

This power is something that nothing else has—not ideas or emotions, not the voice of a person or the shared opinions of people.

Even I don't have complete control over this power in me.

It's not an aggressive power.

It's not trying to get fulfilled or realized.

It's not exactly the power of seduction or allurement, either.

Nothing is accomplished by sex.

If you're looking for something out of it, I don't think you'll get what you're looking for.

Certainly not self-confidence.

It's not the feeling of existing and being alive, exactly.

You cannot even "give" in sex.

There's nothing to give.

It's pleasure without anything further, when it's good.

It's sort of an irresistible desire for close bodily contact.

It's easy to tell when sex is bad: someone is using you when it's bad, someone takes—steals—something from you when it's bad.

When it's good, it's more complicated: you want to feel like a desired *object*, but an object that is an end in itself, that has value (as a body) as itself.

There is romance, of course: there is laughter; there are words; there is honesty; there are questions and answers; there is thought and imagination; there is confession.

But good sex introduces the body as an *object* that is neither mine nor yours: it's almost a spiritual or mystical experience, where you feel like neither subject nor object, neither anything special nor anything small.

I don't know how to describe it.

Maybe you think I'm making too much of it.

Maybe I am.

Maybe you know what I'm talking about or trying to say.

There's something very human about it.

It's a feeling of wanting to be closer than close to someone.

You want to give without taking.

You want to receive without sacrificing anything about yourself.

I'm not sure why, but I think good sex will have a moment of shared laughter in there somewhere, at the beginning, middle, or end—somewhere in there, because of the exceeding pleasure of it.

The romance around it is all the feelings about it.

Good sex has a lot of vulnerability about it.

Of course, maybe I'm talking about ideal sex—or an ideal of sex—instead of "mere" good sex; although I'm not sure this is true.

Even when mathematicians talk about their ideal points and lines and circles and their universal constants, these are not only ideal figures but also real *in a mathematical sense*; even if they don't exist "in reality."

In the same way, what I'm talking about may be ideal, but it's also very much real *in a bodily sense.*

I'm not sure, even if I were the greatest poet or a loving father, I could say it much clearer than I have.

The language just isn't there to talk about good sex.

To talk about bad sex is easy; the things that are bad about bad sex are the same things that make everything bad: people get possessive, exert their power over you, leave you no choice, disrespect you (control your desire), use you as a means to some other end, feel shame about it, and so on.

Love

Love has more to it.

Love is when you know that someone is really thinking about you.

In love, someone will strangely limit her freedom and pleasure for you—to make room for you in a real relationship.

Someone will push herself out of her own way and almost dance with you in love, so to speak: the way planets or moons can orbit around each other.

No one is at the center.

You get pushed off track and are spinning, and suddenly you get a glimpse of how the real world is from a wholly different perspective, in which you fall, in love, as they say.

There're no obvious rules about love, either.

There's almost nothing to be gained in love, either.

I've been caring for a loved one, for example, for some time now.

Not long.

I hope he gets better soon and fast.

I hope he's able to do all the things he used to do soon and fast, like getting out of bed, standing up, and walking, and preparing his meals, and working at his desk, and being an all-around delight, even while being, at the same time, a very difficult person.

Aren't we all?

The thing about caring for a loved one is something tricky:

It takes a long time to learn that the loved one, in his

time of need, is not able to care for you in the same way as before.

The loved one, in his time of need, can hardly care for himself.

There's not enough care sometimes left over in him to spend on you.

It's not all or nothing.

Surely, there are moments when he gets soft and teary, and he crumbles and tells me how much he wants me to be happy and so on.

He tells me he wants me *not* to be sitting by him and spending time with him. (He means: he doesn't want me to *have to* sit by him and *have to* spend time with him — i.e., he wishes he were better and could care for me how he used to.) He tells me he wants me to be out there with my friends and be smart and get smart and have fun and live life, and so on.

I say to him that there's no happiness like that in the world. (He doesn't like to hear me say that.)

I say to him that happiness and sadness go together.

I say to him that sometimes happiness gets in the way of change and learning and simply being.

I say to him that I believe in pleasure, sure; but I believe in goodness instead of happiness. (Maybe that's what I was trying to say when I was talking about good sex.)

I say to him that happiness belongs to him who knows goodness.

My loved one says, "I want you to be happy."

I say to him that "man proposes. God disposes."

He tells me he doesn't want to hear all that.

He asks me if he doesn't have a right to wish me happiness.

I say to him that he has every right; but it doesn't change anything.

He says, "I want you to be cheerful, and joyful, and peaceful."

I say, "Yes."

I say, "Yes, I can do that. I believe in that."

There's nothing to be gained in love: that's what makes love *more than* a feeling.

Love is a bond.

Love takes time.

Love steals time away from me and you and him.

Love is when I understand that I am capable of nothing but love and loving.

That's what separates love from pleasure.

Love totally belongs to the one who loves.

Love doesn't belong to the loved one.

You can't give it.

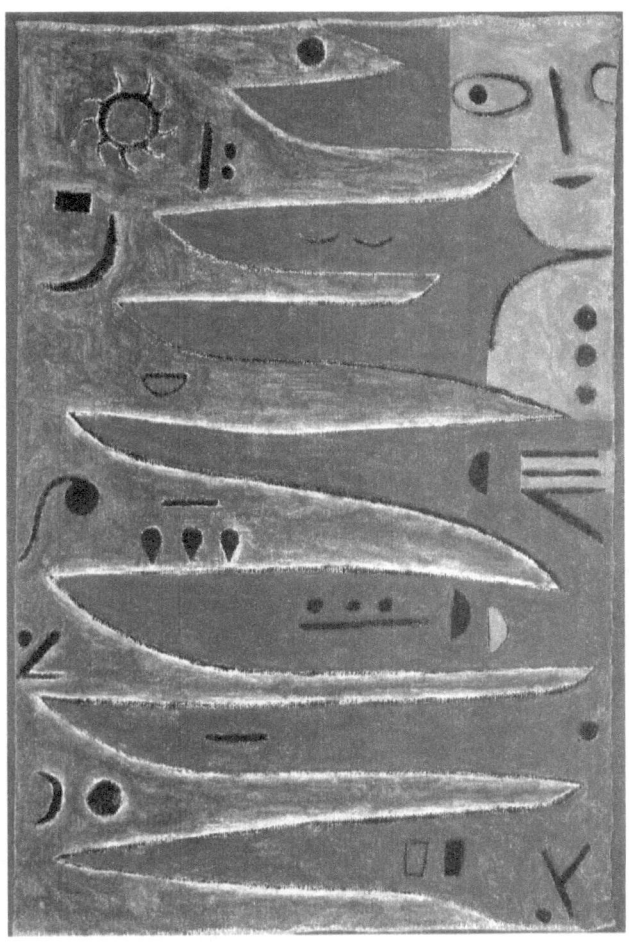

You can fall into it, yes.

It's a complex kind of dance.

I'm not much good at dancing.

I am good at falling.

The best way to be in love—the best way to show your love-feelings, the best way to introduce your love-feelings to someone—is to be embarrassed by your love-feelings.

It's embarrassing.

Here you are.

You have nothing.

But love.

For no reason in particular.

For no reason at all.

For all the reasons.

You can offer nothing.

But love.

It's literally nothing.

And so nothing is gained.

Nothing is given.

Because there is no "why."

There's no reason to love.

Shyam is totally fond of a quote by a Danish dancer who said, "The contradiction which arrests [the understanding] is that a man is required to make the greatest possible sacrifice, to dedicate his whole life as a sacrifice—and wherefore? There is no wherefore. 'Then it is madness,' says the understanding. There is no wherefore, because there is an infinite wherefore."

I don't know what it means.

But love is something like that.

You can't explain it.

Love *is* the explanation.

Shyam says that Eros was a Greek God born of the Void (Chaos, Chasm). In the beginning was the Void, which gave birth to Earth (life-giver, life-giving), Tartarus (a place of no forgiveness), and Eros (love).

Strange, isn't it?

These three things come from nothing.

There is *no greater meaning* to life, suffering, or love *beyond* life, suffering, and love.

Sometimes that's how it is.

There is no guarantee that love will be rewarded.

Love happens out of nowhere.

You feel it has to be; but the truth is—the beauty of it is—it doesn't have to be.

Life happens out of nowhere.

I've often wondered how, in countries and places where there is no end to war and suffering, people go on making families and caring for children. I guess I understand a little now. Sometimes life has to be. Sometimes life goes on making life. It comes out of nowhere. The beauty of it is that it doesn't *have to* be, but it *comes and fights to be, and wants, and gives of itself* so much more than we can offer in return.

Forgiveness happens out of forgiveness.

You almost feel foolish giving forgiveness sometimes.

Maybe it is foolish.

Love is mad, so they say.

So is life and forgiveness.

People get to have the right not to forgive, because forgiveness doesn't have to be.

Isn't there anything greater than love?

I believe so.

Truth, maybe?

Faith.

If you practice truth and faith the way one feels love— like, without asking about *what's in it for me?*—then, you might live a little more free.

You might want to stop making meaning out of everything.

I can't talk about love and not talk about poetry.

I want to understand poetry better and want to understand why I like poetry.

I think I like it, because not everything in poetry makes sense.

Not everything has to mean something.

Sometimes poetry says that it knows nothing about love, even while it has written about nothing other than love.

The strange thing is that I like writing poetry.

I don't like reading it.

I don't think I've ever read a poem and really liked it.*

---

* This is not true. Sanjay reads *Owls and Other Fantasies* by Mary Oliver all the time for fun (personal enjoyment) and for study (to learn how to get better as a writer, what to write

I'm starting to think that poetry is not for readers to like it.

I think that, for one reason or another, the poet wrote it to save her life, to say something that doesn't make sense to anyone—and won't make sense—and that's okay.

I like to write like that.

As if words were saving my life.

I say "as if," because words can't save lives.

Maybe they can; maybe they can't; I don't know.

But they can't, really.

In a funny way, I actually like when poems are not good.

I actually think that most poets know that their poems are not good.

That's why they keep writing and trying.

I actually think that every great poet is embarrassed of every poem she's ever written.

How embarrassing to publish a work of poems!

---

about, how to add feeling to the writing, what topics to write about, and so on). Read the first five sentences of *Owls*, and tell me this whole essay isn't Sanjay's way of saying what the poem is saying.

Who does that?

I like the thought, though.

A good poet, like good love, like good sex, knows that it fails all the time.

When there are no rules—when there can be no rules— of course there will be failure.

There will only be failure.

Take love: you try to say how you feel, and you fail to be able to say how you feel the way you want to say it.

That's love.

Those're poetry's words.

In fact, it's suspicious if you were really good at it: it sounds like "a line" if you're really good at it.

There's something more authentic, more sincere about failing to be able to say the words in the way you wanted.

There's something more soulful about it.

There really is something about speaking from the heart.

When you speak from the heart, you keep all the mistakes in.

You're moved by your own soul, and what is regarded as a defect is your very soul appearing and moving you to say what you don't have all the words to say.

I don't want to say that love always fails.

I do want to say that, even when love fails, it's love.

When your loved one can't care for you, you feel it and it hurts; and yet this is love.

This is still love.

Love belongs to the lover.

Love can't accomplish much.

Love was never meant to.

Love happens when you stop wanting it to save your life.

Love happens when you stop wanting it to make (meaning for) your life.

Poetry happens when you let the words take you to where they want to go.

Poetry happens when you feel the same defect in you that is in the words.

They say that Eros is an immortal God and cannot die.

But Eros can suffer and get disfigured.

Poetry cannot die.

Poetry gets like Eros sometimes.

Love makes you crumble.

Love makes you less.

Love makes you: we all know that.

But less.

Maybe I'm just now remembering two more things that're more important than love: joy and devotion.

I'm remembering them now, because I'm remembering a poem that said:

If you suddenly and unexpectedly feel joy, don't hesitate. Give in to it. There are plenty of lives and whole towns destroyed or about to be. We are not wise, and not very often kind. And much can never be redeemed. Still, life has some possibility left. Perhaps this is its way of fighting back, that sometimes something happens better than all the riches or power in the world. It could be anything, but very likely you notice it in the instant when love begins. Anyway, that's often the case. Anyway, whatever it is, don't be afraid of its plenty. Joy is not made to be a crumb.

I'll come back to this idea.

It's the same idea as Eros being born of Void (Chaos).

Love is a way of fighting back.

Against what?

Against Eros's companions, non-forgiveness and life itself.

I'll come back to this.

Love is a crushing feeling.

You have to be willing to be embarrassed, without the right words, torn apart, pulled in two directions.

I once heard a song that said, "Pull me apart, want you

to see who I am . . . My lover, my light, my destroyer, my meteorite, pull me apart, put me back together."

In the midst of all these feelings, someone my age becomes unsure about what she's all about.

Self-Esteem

In the midst of everything I've said, what happens to a young person's self-image, self-esteem?

You see the problem I'm seeing?

There are x number of songs about falling in love with someone who doesn't see you.

She doesn't know you're there, which makes you feel like you don't exist when you're in her orbit.

You see the problem I'm seeing?

You almost want to be seen, but *as soon as you're seen* by her, you're terrified.

Is love fighting against non-existence? *Or is love fighting back against existing in the first place? Is existence too terrifying? And is love the answer? Is love a way to hide/erase/not face yourself?*

Shyam said that, although many people think Hamlet was around thirty in *Hamlet*, this age seems way too high.

Being thirty was probably an inside joke of Shakespeare's acting troupe. Hamlet might have been in his late teens or early twenties. In any case, Ophelia was for sure in her teens. Jesus's disciples, except for Peter, were classic teenagers, and John was squarely my age. Achilles was probably seventeen when the Trojan War started. Langston Hughes was eighteen when he wrote "The Negro Speaks of Rivers." Plato was twenty-eight when his teacher died.

So, when Hamlet says, "To be, or not to be," someone my age gets it. He's not on the verge of ending his life. He's asking about his self-image, his self-esteem, his dignity, his grace, his goodness. He says that life is a heartache and a "thousand natural shocks." What do you do when you're in between a rock and a hard place? The rock is his feeling that "I did love you once," and the hard place is his inability to forgive the world for being what it is.

What is self-esteem?

What is my self-image?

I'm not sure I'm the best person to speak about all this.

I find that as soon as you really ask yourself, "Who am I?" the next questions are for sure "Why do I exist?" and "Ought I to exist?" or "Why should I exist?"

I'm not going down that path.

These are questions with no answers.

I exist, because I exist for no reason.

I have not written about religion, yet; and I probably won't, here. But I like this idea that we are alive to be devoted and devotional.

We are alive to put ourselves second.

What comes first?

First comes our devotion.

First comes what we do with ourselves.

What we say.

How we speak.

How we move and position our bodies.

It's a private existence.

It's almost an empty existence.

It's a giving existence.

I often feel this way in my own way.

I am a witness.

I feel like a witness.

Even to my devotion, I feel like a witness.

I like to feel small.

I love to feel small.

I love to look at the sky and the clouds, for example, and the colors of the sun and feel that everything I accomplish and write and think and, ultimately, love and feel-loved-by is smaller than the smallest pieces of the sky and clouds I see almost any time during any day at any hour in any mood, even on my biggest days—days that I'll remember for the rest of my life.

I like to see that all this is—all these are—temporary, meant to be only for today at this time, in this moment, and also *for no one in particular* but for the health of the planet.

Isn't that really something?

To be for the health of the planet, the running of the planet, the weather and mood of the planet, so that these people and creatures here can sleep while these people and creatures over there can get going in the morning.

It is all so quiet.

Even rains and storms, I believe, are quiet, more internal—like, a private conversation—than raging, and

more as an outpouring than anything deliberate or intentional.

I guess I live in a state* that has changes of seasons, so I feel this way.

I don't know what it's like to live somewhere where the sky is always raining or sunning or over-oppressive in any manner. Maybe in those places they think differently about being small. Maybe they feel cramped under their hats or large temporary roofs not too far overhead. But, then again, maybe I'm wrong, because whenever I see a sunset I imagine (without intending to do so) that I'm out in the desert, like in New Mexico or Arizona, and I'm free. I'm a rancher, I imagine, of some kind; and I feel the sky very close to me, as if all this sky and openness were for me alone.**

Perhaps when I say I enjoy being small, it really means

---

* New Jersey.
** "At some point in life the world's beauty becomes enough. You don't need to photograph, paint or even remember it. It is enough. No record of it needs to be kept and you don't need someone to share it with or tell it to. When that happens—that letting go—you let go because you can. The world will always be there—while you sleep it will be there—when you wake it will be there as well. So you can sleep and there is reason to wake. A dead hydrangea is as intricate and lovely as one in bloom. Bleak sky is as seductive as sunshine, miniature orange trees without blossom or fruit are not defective; they are that." Toni Morrison, *Tar Baby*.

that I like the feeling of aloneness.

What is self-esteem?

Self-esteem is about being alone.

Self-esteem is about being temporary.

How do I see myself?

At my age, I am change.

At your age, so are you but heavier.*

Self-esteem—i.e., believing yourself to be somebody—comes from absolutely nothing, for no reason.

Self-esteem is saying, "I have the ability to change the conditions of my life: to take action and do something about myself."

I'm sorry to say this, but this is what Ophelia was trying to do and say all through the *Hamlet* play. She's the one who said that the question isn't "to be or not to be." She said the question is: "We know what we are, but what may we be?"

She sings a song a lot like the song I was thinking of before: "I think you've mistaken," she says, "my desperation for devotion. Don't mistake my breaking

---

* "Can't nobody fly with all that shit. Wanna fly, you got to give up the shit that weighs you down." Toni Morrison, *Song of Solomon*.

open for broken."

I may not be the best person to talk about self-esteem and self-image.

I want to be changeful and open.

I don't want to have an opinion of myself.

If I really think about it, I'll come up with the usual awful things: how I wish I were more attractive in my body, how I wish I were more seductive and alluring, how I wish I could read the signs and signals better about what people are telling me.

These all have to do with relationships.

I suppose I wish I were better at relationships.

I suppose I wish I were better at intimate conversation.

I suppose so did Ophelia.

Did she try to change the conditions of her life?

Yes.

Did she take action?

Sadly, yes.

Did she have this feeling that I sometimes have that all this is temporary and alone?

I don't think so.

Remember the poem about "Joy is not made to be a crumb" from before?

Well, very often, joy is *not* the instant when love begins, as Ophelia knew all too well.

Sometimes joy is in the *pure fighting back against life when fighting makes no sense at all.*

I sometimes feel like Hamlet and Ophelia were the same person with only one difference: Hamlet, at least, *pretended* to be suffering from madness *so that he wouldn't*

actually go through it into complete madness.

There's something* to be said about that.

He was acting out, sure.

He was cruel and unkind, for certain.

It's not kind to pretend to be someone you're not with someone you love.

It's better to speak from the heart—and not pretend—when you're in front of someone you love.

Hamlet's cruelty was that he pretended that he didn't want anything from Ophelia.

That's not a good feeling.

We want someone to want something from us.

Even when I know I don't have it—whatever "it" is, maybe love, joy, sexuality, desire, openness, infinite possibility—I want him to want it of me.

That's the trick of self-esteem.

Self-esteem is supposed to be a relationship with myself.

But self-esteem really is wanting to be asked by another person for something I don't have, so that I have the desire to go get it for myself (often from you). *Self-esteem*

---

* Something positive.

is wanting a reason for me to take action by myself and put myself in motion. *Self-esteem is finding out all the things you don't have in order to hand them over to you (who, more often than not, don't want it).*

Self-esteem is a willingness-to-be for many reasons, not just one reason.

In any case, self-esteem doesn't go up and down, as if it were counting out dips and swells in mood. It's more about *what can I do with myself? And a willingness to try. A belief in trials-and-trying and a willingness to lose, and go on, and find a way on.*

Transition to Adulthood

What do I think about becoming older?

What do I think about adulthood, and independence and self-sufficiency?

This'll be the last topic of this essay.

I don't think much about it.

I don't see anyone I truly admire in public life.

I don't see anyone of whom I'm jealous about any part of her life.

I see that most adults have a major tragedy looming in

a serious part of their lives that they are simply avoiding and keeping quiet about.

What do I want for myself in the future?

Financial independence and self-sufficiency are no joke. I'm not downplaying them. I think it's good to know that you have money enough to run away from your life if you ever needed to. I think it's good to know that you can start over again, no matter what happens. An older brother of a friend of mine once told me the best thing his father (now passed) told him: the father said, "You have good hands." The father was a carpenter, and he was teaching the son how to be a carpenter. "So long as you hold on to your hands, you'll be okay; you can make money with your hands; you'll be alright."

I like that idea.

I remember one time I met a sitar player named V. N. Seshadri, and she shook my hand when I put out my hand. I thought that was special. I thought that the artist's whole life and career were her hands, and she let me have them for a moment. But then someone asked me, "Isn't everyone's whole life and career in her hands?" I guess, maybe.

But I guess what I admired is that the older brother and sitar player were dedicated to something other than sitting in front of a computer. Sometimes I've seen doctors and nurses—for nurses, I have the highest

regard, beyond comparison by far—working at their computers for most of their workday. I guess writers sit at their computers, too, mostly. I once heard an honest confession by an author who said he did a lot of his research on Pinterest, finding there old newspaper articles and photos. (I remember, in a very different context, Shyam was telling me that Colson Whitehead first heard about the Dozier School from Twitter, and then he went to libraries to read as much as he could about the people and their lives. Whitehead wanted to go to the place itself in Florida, but he felt he couldn't bear the evilness of the place and thought it would literally bring pain and harm to himself and his psyche. I get that. I bring it up only because I thought the movie *The Nickel Boys* should have won best picture this year. It's a movie I never will forget, and the faces of the kids I will never forget, nor their names, Elwood and Turner.)

I wonder if people my age think more about circumstances than transitioning into adulthood.

What does it mean to be an adult?

The transition (path) would be easy if the end were clear.

If an adult is someone who cares for others, then that's something people my age already know how to do. We know how to forgive, too, and offer more chances than you'd expect to come your way.

If an adult is someone who wants to give back to others, maybe we worry about how we got what we got more than we worry about if we'll have enough for ourselves.

People my age may be idealistic.

I, for sure, am idealistic.

I'm borderline dreamy.

I'm borderline delusional, you might say. (And yet, I feel okay about it all. Are you okay with all your delusions?)

And someone like me has the hardest path to adulthood, for I don't respect many of the conditions that make adulthood. I don't know why preexisting conditions play such a huge factor in having some of the basic comforts of life. A friend of mine once asked me why the world is so beautiful for some—and they have the time to enjoy that beauty—while for others the world is cruel and bitter and hateful. I had no other answer than "luck," an answer I'm not very happy with.

It may not be such a bad thing for the transition to adulthood to be so hard for young people like me nowadays. I feel people my age have a greater feeling for youth, honestly. (I actually totally honestly believe that all generations are one and the same: no difference whatsoever. Older people and old people like to fabricate a romantic story about their lives, often a complete lie through and through. Why should my generation be any different?)

I was trying to say earlier that I don't wish to work for the rest of my life in front of a computer; I don't know how I'll manage that.

Perhaps people my age want to take action but don't

know how exactly.

What do I imagine for myself?

Ideally, I imagine that I may be of great service to this world. By *world*, I mean maybe I'll be able to tell the truth about myself to people and not be ashamed about myself and the choices I may make. By *world*, I mean the people I may end up working with and having conversations with.

I wish to find joy in lots of different things that have nothing to do with news and politics, like music and movies; I want to learn how to draw and paint and illustrate and design; I want to be okay being alone; I want people to know what I know and don't know; I want to meet someone who has found some answers about how to live, and who isn't selling her knowledge, or selling anything.

I haven't spoken about a lot of things in this essay.

It is nonetheless time to conclude.

I couldn't get to everything.

I won't *conclude* conclude.

I'll just say things:

Young people care about the environment and the way we care for and treat the animals.

Young people think about how to be fair to each other and stay out of each other's way.

Young people dream of revenge but won't go through with it.

Young people, I guess, at their best, are no different from Ophelia, John, Langston, and a very young Plato, whose lives were touched by grief.

Young people do not believe in suffering in silence.

Dear young people, don't suffer in silence!

Young people do not believe in living in fear.

We do not want to be afraid.

We will live.

And we will remember the ones who died too early, too.

And for all this, I would not mind asking for your help, dear reader.

If you do not believe in what I've said, or do not wish to help, then stay out of my way.

I know that I'm not perfect.

You're not perfect.

Nothing is perfect.

No one is perfect, I know that. We're all more often than not faint, weak, tired, timid, irresolute, dependent, lonely, crumbly, rough, first-draft, secondhand, secondary creatures, which is great. I love that. That is just what it is.

The last literary works Shyam and I read together were the letters of John the Apostle. We read them to learn how to write nice, short sentences, get to the point, get the point across, and get out. John writes about all the things you would think a man like him would write about; but he also has a few words of warning against listening to people who are angry all the time and who promote themselves instead of any greater (infinite) idea to which they've dedicated their lives.

I feel pretty certain that John was writing to people my age. He was writing to and thinking about himself as he was when he first came to life (spiritually, as it were).

Young people do not like to be in the company of older people who live in despair and wish for us to quiet down and mind our place.

We have faith in ourselves, and we, I imagine, will be tested in our faith.

I conclude by saying: I will do something with my life. I want to change the circumstances that weigh on young people like me.

It's not impossible.

And you will not like it if you get in my way.

The End

Acknowledgments
by Shyam Gohel

I thank everyone who made this book possible.

I thank Sanjay most of all.

I dedicate this work to academic teachers who believed in me, and who, therefore, were tough as nails on me:

All through my youth, my music teachers Mohan Deshpande and John Ketterer taught me that learning could be fun, loud, challenging, serious, and joyful. Education isn't only the process of learning but the development of endowments into talents and the exercise of those talents, i.e., a lot of practice. And the results speak for themselves. No one wants to hear it if it's unpleasant.

At South Brunswick High School, NJ, my English and Film Studies teacher Harry Schultz was the epitome of academic discipline and human compassion. I remember his influence on me every single day.

At NYU, Robert Gurland and Victoria Blythe spent so much time with me. I ended up taking an independent study with each of them every semester, which filled up half my course load. Seth Benardete and Elias Khoury were also very generous to me. I walked into their office hours every chance I had; and they actually listened to me, even though (even I knew) I had no idea what I was (talking) about.

At The New School, Dmitri Nikulin, Richard J. Bernstein, and Agnes Heller kept pushing me to speak up and come out of my shell. They were honest with me and treated me with respect. I think of some of their encouraging words to me to this very day. Richard J. Bernstein was especially challenging as a teacher. He set high standards and never gave me the impression that, if I worked hard and kept asking questions and kept being vulnerable about my ignorance and open to learning, I couldn't fulfill them.

"Live for an ideal, and that one ideal alone. Let it be so great, so strong, that there may be nothing else left in the mind; no place for anything else, no time for anything else." "That is the one great first step—the real desire for the ideal. (Everything comes easy after that.) The struggle is the great lesson. Mind you, the great benefit in this life is struggle."

Credit: The poem on page 72 is "Don't Hesitate" by Mary Oliver. Reprinted by the permission of The Charlotte Sheedy Literary Agency as agent for the author. Copyright © 2010, 2017 by Mary Oliver with permission of Bill Reichblum.

Source: The quotations on page 26 are from Gillian Rose. *Love's Work*. New York Review of Books, 1995.

Source: The quotation on page 65 is from Søren Kierkegaard. *Training in Christianity*. Princeton University Press, 1972.

Source: The song quoted on pages 72–73 is from Cassandra Jenkins. "Omakase." *My Light, My Destroyer*. Dead Oceans, Inc., 2024.

Source: The song quoted on pages 79–80 is from Cassandra Jenkins. "Devotion." *My Light, My Destroyer*. Dead Oceans, Inc., 2024.

Illustrations: All paintings and sketches inside this book are by Paul Klee (1879 – 1940).

Cover art: Paul Klee. *Pierrot Lunaire*, 1924.

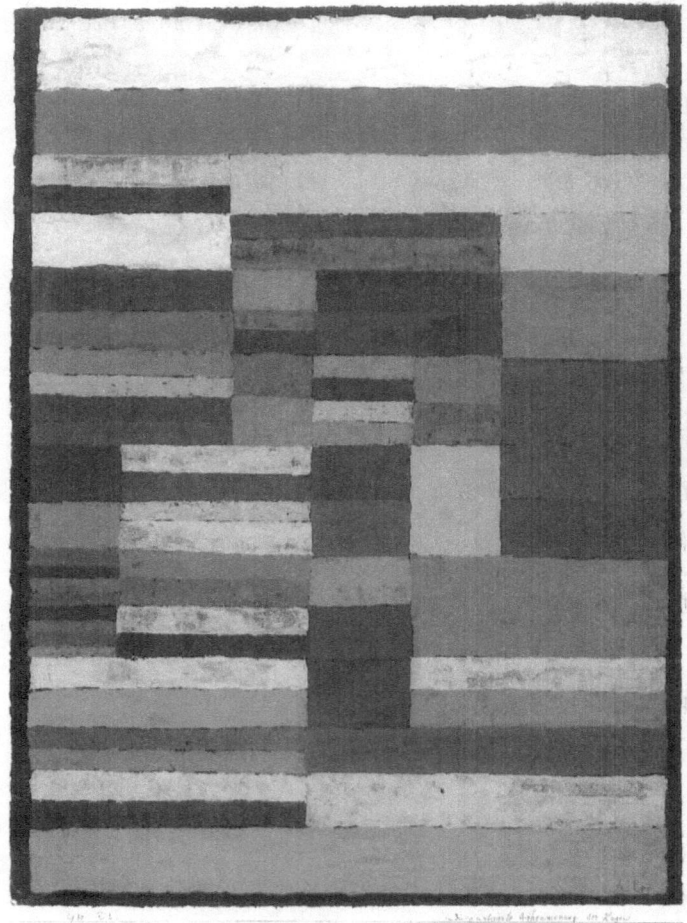

About the Authors

Sanjay has moved on from English and reading classes. He is receiving other tuition classes from some of my colleagues: painting lessons from Erica Holliday, film studies with Jillian Stein, and soccer practice with Kenneth Tsui. Sanjay dedicates this essay to his new teachers.

Shyam R. Gohel (b. April 1, 1982) may one day resume some of the projects that were started with the teachers mentioned in the Acknowledgments section. Truth be told, Shyam's writing right now is more of a soliloquy "to be or not to be" situation—writing for the sake of the pure creative act of it—and less of a dialogue with competing forms of thought about what it means to live the good life in community with other beings, other creatures (the animals), and things (the health of the planet).

Shyam continues to work on the *Samira Is Wind* novel and a book of poetry, as well as a revenge story (about hurt feelings, lost relationships, and the grief that follows) for teenage readers.

Books by Shyam Gohel

Rana Spring Summer Fall

Asha Deep in My Heart Someday

Samira Is Wind (forthcoming)

Sanjay's Essay on What It's Like to Be Young Today
(for ages 13 – 18)

Nikhil the Noir Detective (ages 8 – 10)

Closed Circle Open World (ages 8 – 10)

Mena, 9 Years Old, in Therapy (ages 8 – 10)

Be Present You're a Present (ages 5 – 9)

1 2 3 4 Let's Be Mindful (ages 3 – 7)

Laugh Before You Sleep (ages 3 – 7)

I Don't Cry for No Reason (ages 3 – 7)

Want a Friend Be a Friend (ages 3 – 7)

Breathe In the Sun Breathe Out a Song (ages 3 – 7)

Why Do I Love? Why Do I Get Upset? (ages 3 – 7)

There's a Flower in Your Heart (ages 3 – 7)

www.ingramcontent.com/pod-product-compliance
Lightning Source LLC
Chambersburg PA
CBHW030642130626
46552CB00002B/978